CHURCHILL DOWNS

The Adventures of Churchill Charlie

CHARLIE LEARNS HE'S SPECIAL

WRITTEN BY
Kelley Cassity

ILLUSTRATED BY
Mike Prather

Published by Churchill Downs Incorporated in association with Moonlight Press
All rights reserved. First edition.
Written by Kelley Cassity
Text © 2001 Churchill Downs Incorporated
Churchill Charlie ® is trademarked by Churchill Downs Incorporated
Illustrations and Book Design by Mike Prather
Illustration © 2001 by Prather Design
ISBN# 0-9709639-0-4

To learn more about Churchill Charlie and the Junior Jockey Club, visit
kentuckyderby.com

Corporate and volume discounts or additional orders are available through:
CD Promotions
P.O. Box 4865
Louisville, KY 40204
502-473-1036

For inquiries regarding original illustrations contact:
Prather Design - 502-491-9000
prather-design.com

Printed by Hamilton Printing
1703 South Brook Street, Louisville, Kentucky 40208

CHARLIE LOVED HIS JOB AT CHURCHILL DOWNS RACETRACK. EVERYDAY HE WOULD PLAY GAMES WITH THE MANY CHILDREN WHO CAME TO VISIT. THE CHILDREN ALL CALLED HIM CHURCHILL CHARLIE. BUT DEEP INSIDE CHARLIE WAS WORRIED BECAUSE HE WASN'T LIKE ALL THE OTHER HORSES AT THE RACETRACK.

"ALL OF THE OTHER HORSES ARE RACEHORSES," CHARLIE THOUGHT TO HIMSELF. "I SHOULD BE A RACEHORSE TOO."

CHURCHILL CHARLIE HAD SEEN THE OTHER HORSES GET READY FOR A RACE. THEY WOULD
MARCH LIKE SOLDIERS ON TO THE TRACK. ONE BY ONE THEY WOULD LOAD INTO A GATE. LIKE MAGIC
THE GATE WOULD BURST OPEN AND THE HORSES WOULD CHARGE AROUND THE TRACK. THEY WOULD
RUN SO FAST THAT THEIR HOOVES WOULD SLING DIRT HIGH INTO THE AIR. BUT TO CHARLIE, THE BEST
PART OF ALL WAS WHEN ALL THE PEOPLE WOULD LEAP TO THEIR FEET AND CHEER AS THE HORSES RAN BY.

"ALL THEY HAVE TO DO IS RUN AROUND THE TRACK. I CAN DO THAT. THAT'S EASY," THOUGHT CHARLIE. "THEN, THE CROWD WILL CHEER FOR ME."

CHARLIE TOLD THE CHILDREN HIS NEW PLAN. THEY ALL WISHED HIM LUCK AND CHURCHILL CHARLIE WENT TO WORK TO BECOME A RACEHORSE.

But Charlie didn't know the first thing about becoming a racehorse. Then he remembered that the racehorses live in stables behind the racetrack.

"I'll go there and ask for help. Maybe the other horses can tell me how to be a racehorse," Charlie thought.

CHARLIE FOUND THE STABLES. THERE WERE ROWS AND ROWS OF BARNS FILLED WITH RACEHORSES. CHARLIE STOPPED AT THE FIRST BARN WHERE HE SAW A LARGE BLACK HORSE WITH A WHITE STAR ON HIS FOREHEAD. THE HORSE LOOKED VERY STRONG.

"I BET HE'S VERY FAST," THOUGHT CHARLIE. "I'LL ASK HIM FOR HELP."

"EXCUSE ME. I WANT TO BE A RACEHORSE. CAN YOU TELL ME HOW?" CHARLIE ASKED.

BUT THE HORSE DIDN'T SPEAK. THE HORSES IN THE BARN WERE ALL LINED UP EATING THEIR HAY. NO ONE PAID ANY ATTENTION TO CHARLIE'S REQUEST. SO CHARLIE SPOKE LOUDER.

"EXCUSE ME! I'M SORRY TO INTERRUPT, BUT I WANT TO BE A RACEHORSE. I WAS HOPING YOU WOULD HELP ME."

THE HORSES LOOKED UP AT CHURCHILL CHARLIE AND BURST INTO LAUGHTER. THEY
WHINNIED, THEY NEIGHED AND STOMPED THEIR HOOVES. THEY LAUGHED SO HARD AND SO LONG
THEIR SIDES BEGAN TO ACHE.

CHARLIE DIDN'T UNDERSTAND.

"WHAT IS SO FUNNY? WHY WON'T YOU HELP ME?"

CHARLIE BEGAN TO WALK AWAY WHEN THE BLACK HORSE WITH A WHITE STAR SPOKE.

"DON'T YOU KNOW? YOU CANNOT BE A RACEHORSE," SAID THE BLACK HORSE WITH A WHITE STAR.

"AND WHY NOT?" ASKED CHARLIE VERY PUZZLED.

"YOU ARE NOT A THOROUGHBRED. WE ARE ALL THOROUGHBRED RACEHORSES. YOU CANNOT POSSIBLY RUN AS SWIFTLY AS A THOROUGHBRED."

"Oh yes I can," replied Charlie. "I mean, I've never really tried, but it looks easy. I know I can do it."

"Who is your trainer?" asked the black horse with a white star.

"What is a trainer?" asked Charlie.

"Dear boy, every racehorse has a trainer. He watches a stopwatch and tells us how quickly we are running. Then, we tell him in which races we wish to run."

"I don't have one of those," said Charlie.

"Do you have an exercise rider?" the experienced black horse with a white star asked.

"No. What do they do?" asked Charlie.

"Racehorses let exercise riders ride on our backs each morning while we run, so that they can see what it's like to run fast. I don't suppose I even need to ask if you have a saddle."

Charlie looked at the ground and shook his head no.

"VERY WELL," SAID THE EXPERIENCED HORSE. "TOMORROW YOU TRAIN WITH ME."
THE OTHER HORSES IN THE BARN GASPED. FOR EVERYONE, EXCEPT CHURCHILL CHARLIE,
KNEW THAT THE BLACK HORSE WITH A WHITE STAR WAS NOT AN ORDINARY RACEHORSE. HE WAS A
CHAMPION AND THE FASTEST HORSE IN THE ENTIRE BARN.

THE NEXT MORNING THE BLACK HORSE WITH A WHITE STAR NUDGED CHARLIE.
"WAKE UP. IF YOU WANT TO BE A RACEHORSE, YOU MUST GET UP EARLY. BREAKFAST IS AT 4 A.M."

AFTER BREAKFAST, ALL THE HORSES FROM ALL THE BARNS BEGAN TO LINE UP. ONE BY ONE THEY WENT TO THE TRACK FOR THEIR MORNING WORKOUT. EACH TIME A TRAINER WAS THERE WITH A STOPWATCH, JUST LIKE THE BLACK HORSE HAD SAID. WHEN THE BLACK HORSE WITH A WHITE STAR STEPPED ON TO THE TRACK, THE OTHER HORSES GOT VERY QUIET. FIRST, HE STARTED TO TROT, THEN GALLOP, AND THEN HE RAN SO FAST CHARLIE COULD HARDLY SEE HIS HOOVES HIT THE DIRT. HE WAS THE FASTEST OF THEM ALL.

THE MAN WITH THE STOPWATCH SMILED.

"WAY TO GO," HE YELLED.

CHURCHILL CHARLIE COULDN'T WAIT. HE STEPPED ON TO THE TRACK. IT WASN'T EVEN HIS TURN, BUT HE JUST HAD TO START RUNNING. HE RAN HARDER AND FASTER THAN HE HAD EVER RUN BEFORE. CHARLIE WAS SO PROUD. HE IMAGINED HE WAS RUNNING IN A REAL RACE.

"I'M REALLY RACING AND ALL THE PEOPLE WILL LEAP TO THEIR FEET AND CHEER FOR ME."

But when he stopped running and looked up, all the other horses were laughing.

"That's the slowest horse I've ever seen," yelled the man with the watch. "Get off the track."

The black horse with a white star just turned away.

Charlie was so embarrassed he couldn't move. Men surrounded Charlie, grabbed his mane and pulled him off the track.

"I DON'T UNDERSTAND," SAID CHARLIE. "I RAN AS FAST AS I COULD."
CHURCHILL CHARLIE WALKED SLOWLY BACK TO THE BARN. HE COULDN'T BEAR TO SEE THE
BLACK HORSE WITH A WHITE STAR. CHARLIE KNEW HE WOULD NEVER SPEAK TO HIM AGAIN.

JUST THEN HE HEARD A FAMILIAR VOICE.

"DO YOU KNOW WHO I AM?" THE BLACK HORSE WITH THE WHITE STAR ASKED.

"NO," CHARLIE SAID SOFTLY.

"I AM A CHAMPION Thoroughbred. I AM ONE OF THE FASTEST HORSES AT THE RACETRACK. DO YOU KNOW WHY?"

"BECAUSE YOU'RE BETTER THAN ME," CHARLIE SAID.

"No. Absolutely not," said the black horse with a white star. "I was born a Thoroughbred. I was born to be a racehorse."

"YOU ARE NOT A RACEHORSE. YOU ARE CHURCHILL CHARLIE," SAID THE BLACK HORSE.

"HOW DID YOU KNOW MY NAME?" CHARLIE WAS AMAZED.

"MY DEAR BOY, EVERYONE KNOWS YOUR NAME. YOU ARE FAMOUS."

"I AM?" CHARLIE COULDN'T BELIEVE HIS EARS.

"Of course you are. There are many racehorses here at the track, but only one horse gets to play games with all the children and that is you. The children love you and that's what makes you so special."

THE BLACK HORSE WITH A WHITE STAR WAS RIGHT. CHURCHILL CHARLIE WAS SO EXCITED. HE THANKED THE BLACK HORSE FOR ALL HIS WISDOM AND RAN TO THE OTHER SIDE OF THE TRACK TO FIND THE CHILDREN, FASTER THAN HE HAD EVER RUN BEFORE.

But by the time Charlie found the children, he was so out of breath he couldn't speak. The children turned around and leaped to their feet.

"Churchill Charlie!" They all yelled and ran to greet him.

Churchill Charlie smiled. Not only does he get cheers, he gets hugs too.

The End